THE NORTH POLICE

The North Police are

the elves who solve crimes

at the North Pole.

These are their stories . . .

BY
SCOTT SONNEBORN

ILLUSTRATED BY
OMAR LOZANO

THE

NORTH POLICE

Elf Detectives

CAPSTONE YOUNG READERS
A CAPSTONE IMPRINT

The North Police is published by
Capstone Young Readers
a Capstone Imprint
1710 Roe Crest Drive
North Mankato, Minnesota 56003
www.mycapstone.com

Cataloging-in-Publication Data is available at the Library of Congress website.
ISBN: 978-1-62370-838-2 (US paperback)
ISBN: 978-1-62370-839-9 (eBook)

First published as four library-bound hardcover editions:
Reindeer Games (978-1-4795-6487-3); The Mystery of Santa's Sleigh
(978-1-4795-6484-2); Computer Meltdown (978-1-4795-6485-9);
Meet the South Police (978-1-4795-6486-6)

Printed and bound in China.
010342F17

THE NORTH POLICE

CHAPTER 1
Red-nosed Reindeer

It was a bright, cold morning in Christmas Town.

In the North Police station, the chief shouted, "Detectives Sprinkles and Sugarplum! Get in my office! Now!"

Sitting beside the chief was an unhappy reindeer. He had a shiny red snout.

"What happened to your nose?" asked Sugarplum.

"I was playing in the Reindeer Games," said the reindeer. "Then — WHAM! — someone bopped me with a snowboard. I lost the race and got this red mark."

"Now they won't let this red-nosed reindeer join in any Reindeer Games," the chief told Sprinkles and Sugarplum. "Competing hurt is against the rules."

"Whoever wins the Games joins Donner, Blitzen, and the others pulling Santa's sleigh," said the reindeer. "I was in first place."

"Do you think another
reindeer knocked you out of
the Games on purpose?" asked
Detective Sugarplum. "This
case sounds stickier than a wet
candy cane!"

"That's why I'm putting my two best detectives on the case," the chief replied. "I'm sending you both to the Reindeer Games . . . undercover!"

CHAPTER 2
Reindeer Games

At the Games, two reindeer raced on skates. Another pair wrestled with their antlers.

One reindeer swayed on wobbly legs.

"Hey, look at him!" said a mean-looking reindeer, pointing at the wobbly one.

All the other reindeer laughed and called him names.

They didn't know it, but there was a good reason the wobbly reindeer couldn't stand straight. It was the North Police in disguise!

"I don't know if this plan will work," said Sprinkles. "We can't even stand, much less play Reindeer Games!"

"That's why it's going to work." Sugarplum smiled.

The mean reindeer slid over on her snowboard. "Let's race," she said. "You look like you'll be easy to beat!"

The North Police tried to climb onto a snowboard.

"Whoa!" cried Sugarplum and Sprinkles. They slipped and fell into the snow.

"This isn't fair," Detective Sprinkles told the mean reindeer. "You'll win easily."

"I don't care about fair!" said the mean reindeer. "I just want to win!"

Lying on the ground, the North Police saw the bottom of the reindeer's snowboard.

It was bright red — except for a nose-shaped mark of missing paint.

"We caught you red-handed!" said Sugarplum.

ZIPPP! The elves removed their disguise.

"The North Police!" the mean reindeer shouted.

And with that, she flew into the air!

CHAPTER 3
The Saint Nick of Time

"Roasted chestnuts!" shouted Sprinkles, watching the reindeer zoom away.

Sugarplum flashed her badge. Then she hitched a ride on a nearby reindeer.

The North Police detectives WHOOOOSHED through the sky. Soon, they spotted the suspect.

"I'm getting too old for this!" cried Sprinkles.

"Don't be silly," replied Sugarplum. "You're only three hundred and twelve."

She grabbed Sprinkles's arm and jumped!

The North Police landed right atop the mean reindeer. Sugarplum slapped her cuffs on the reindeer's legs.

"We did it!" cried Detective Sprinkles.

"You did it, all right!" said the mean reindeer. "I can't fly with handcuffs on!"

"Ahhh!" they all shouted, tumbling out of the sky.

"Ho, ho, hold on!" cried a voice. It was Santa!

He caught the North Police
and the reindeer in his sleigh.
"Looks like I got here in the
Saint Nick of time!" he said.

"Thanks, Santa," said
Detective Sprinkles.

"Thank you," said Santa. "Without you, I would've had a cheater pulling my sleigh this Christmas."

"Just doing our jobs," said Sugarplum.

"Hooray for the North Police!" said Santa.

"Hooray!" everyone shouted out with glee.

CHAPTER 1
Scratched!

The Christmas Town garage is where Santa's sleigh was stored.

It was also a crime scene!

Santa's sleigh had a huge scratch on it.

Someone must have taken the sleigh out last night and scraped it on something.

Santa couldn't have taken the sleigh out. He had been in bed with a cold.

So who did it?

The North Police's greatest detectives were on the case!

As Detective Sugarplum sipped eggnog, Detective Sprinkles got to work.

Sprinkles dusted for prints with powdered sugar.

But there were no fingerprints at all.

"Hmm," said Sugarplum,  "if someone rode the sleigh last night, he should have left prints. Let's talk to the elf who called about the crime."

Eve's job was to look after

Santa's sleigh.

"What can you tell us, Eve?" asked Sugarplum.

"Only one elf was near the garage," Eve said. "Elfis."

CHAPTER 2
Elfis

Elfis was the coolest elf in Christmas Town.

The North Police found him rocking out on his electric bell at a nearby eggnog hangout.

"You were seen near
the garage last night," said
Detective Sprinkles.

"I'm not talking," Elfis said.

"Then you leave us no
choice," said Sugarplum.

"We're going to have to play good cop, better cop," added Sugarplum.

"Go ahead and try," Elfis said. "Do your best."

"Maybe this will change your mind," said Sprinkles. He held out a bag of candy.

"Jelly beans!" Elfis drooled.

"If you want the beans, you gotta spill the beans," explained Sugarplum.

"I admit it!" said Elfis, grabbing the jelly beans. "I did it! I lost Mrs. Claws!"

"What are you talking about?" asked Sprinkles.

"Santa's cat! I lost her!" said Elfis. "I went looking for her near the garage."

"So you didn't take the sleigh out for a ride?" asked Detective Sprinkles.

"No!" said Elfis.

"Looks like we're out of clues." Sprinkles sighed.

"I don't think so," said Sugarplum. "I think Elfis just gave us another one!"

CHAPTER 3
Case Closed

The detectives returned to the scene of the crime.

"I bet the sleigh got scratched on the North Pole," said Sprinkles. "That pole is pretty pointy!"

"But I don't understand how someone could have gotten the sleigh out of the garage last night without being seen," Sprinkles said.

"I don't think anyone took out the sleigh," said Sugarplum.

"Then how did it get scratched on the North Pole?" asked Sprinkles.

"It wasn't scratched by
the North Pole," replied
Sugarplum. "Was it, girl?"

"Um, I'm not a girl," replied
a very confused Detective
Sprinkles.

"No, you're not," said Detective Sugarplum, "but she is!" She reached behind the sleigh and pulled out . . .

A cat!

It was Mrs. Claws!

"You scratched the sleigh," said Detective Sugarplum as she petted the cat, "didn't you, girl?"

"Meow," said Mrs. Claws.

"Another case neatly wrapped!" the detectives exclaimed.

The North Police had done it again!

Santa was feeling better and happy to have the case solved. He was even happier to have his cat back.

Santa gave Mrs. Claws a jolly old hug.

"Achooo!" he sneezed.

"Sir," said Sprinkles, "maybe you have allergies."

"Another mystery for the North Police!" said Sugarplum.

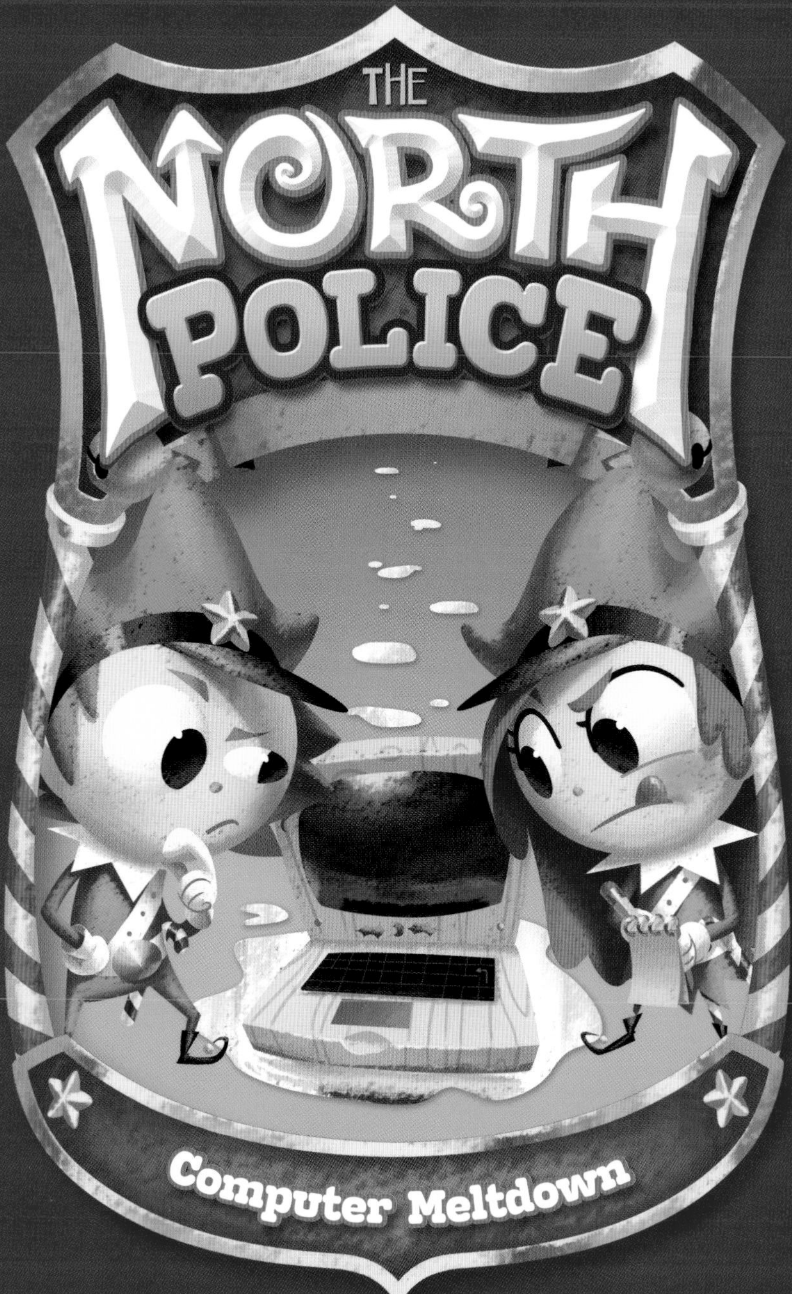
THE
NORTH
POLICE
Computer Meltdown

CHAPTER 1
Santa's Computer

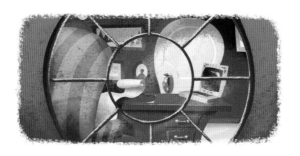

Inside Santa's workshop was a computer. Every day, Santa sat at this computer. Every day, he added names to his naughty and nice lists.

But not today . . .

Santa's computer was missing!

"It was here yesterday," Santa told the North Police's two greatest detectives. "Now there's just a puddle."

"Christmas is tomorrow," said Santa sadly. "How will I know who should get presents without my lists? You've got to find out what happened to my computer!"

 "Maybe the computer had a meltdown," said Detective Sprinkles. "It is rather warm in here."

"I've never heard of a computer melting into water," said Detective Sugarplum. "But there's one way to find out if that's what happened."

"To the lab!" Sprinkles said.

The North Police placed the water in a small baggy.

"To all a good night crime solving!" exclaimed Santa as the North Police left.

CHAPTER 2
The North Police Lab

At the lab, Sprinkles and Sugarplum waited. Their lil' helper elf tested the water.

First, he poured the water into a test tube. Then he put it under a microscope.

"So is it water?" asked Detective Sprinkles.

The lil' helper lifted the test tube and drank the contents.

"Melted snow, to be precise," said the scientist.

"Melted snow!" shouted
Detective Sugarplum. "Let's
take another look at the crime
scene, Sprinkles. I might know
what happened to Santa's
computer!"

CHAPTER 3
Cold Case

The two North Police detectives returned to the scene of the crime.

"Look," said Sugarplum, pointing at the floor. "There's more water over here."

"So?" replied Sprinkles. "It's just melted snow."

"Exactly!" said Detective Sugarplum. "And look where it leads . . ."

The puddles of water led right to the bathrooms.

There were three bathrooms: the Women's Room, the Men's Room, and the Snowmen's Room.

WHAM! WHAM! Detective
Sugarplum knocked on the
door to the Snowmen's Room.

"Open up!" she said. "It's
the North Police!"

There was no answer.

"If there's a snowman in there, button up your coal buttons," said Sugarplum. "We're coming in!"

The two elves burst into the Snowmen's Room.

"Brrr," said Sprinkles. "This isn't like any other bathroom I've ever seen."

"That's because you're not a snowman," said a voice.

The two North Police detectives turned and saw a snowman. He was holding Santa's computer!

"How did you know I took it?" asked the snowman.

"The melted snow," said Detective Sugarplum. "That's what gave you away."

The snowman nodded.

"It was so hot in Santa's Workshop that I started to melt," the snowman said. "So I grabbed the computer and brought it here."

"I knew taking the computer was wrong, but I did it anyway," the snowman said. "I just had to know if my name was on Santa's list!"

"Well, you're definitely on Santa's list now," said Detective Sprinkles.

"Really?" asked the snowman. "Naughty or nice?"

Sugarplum handcuffed the snowman. "I'll let you figure that out," she said.

The North Police smiled.

"Another case neatly wrapped!" they cheered.

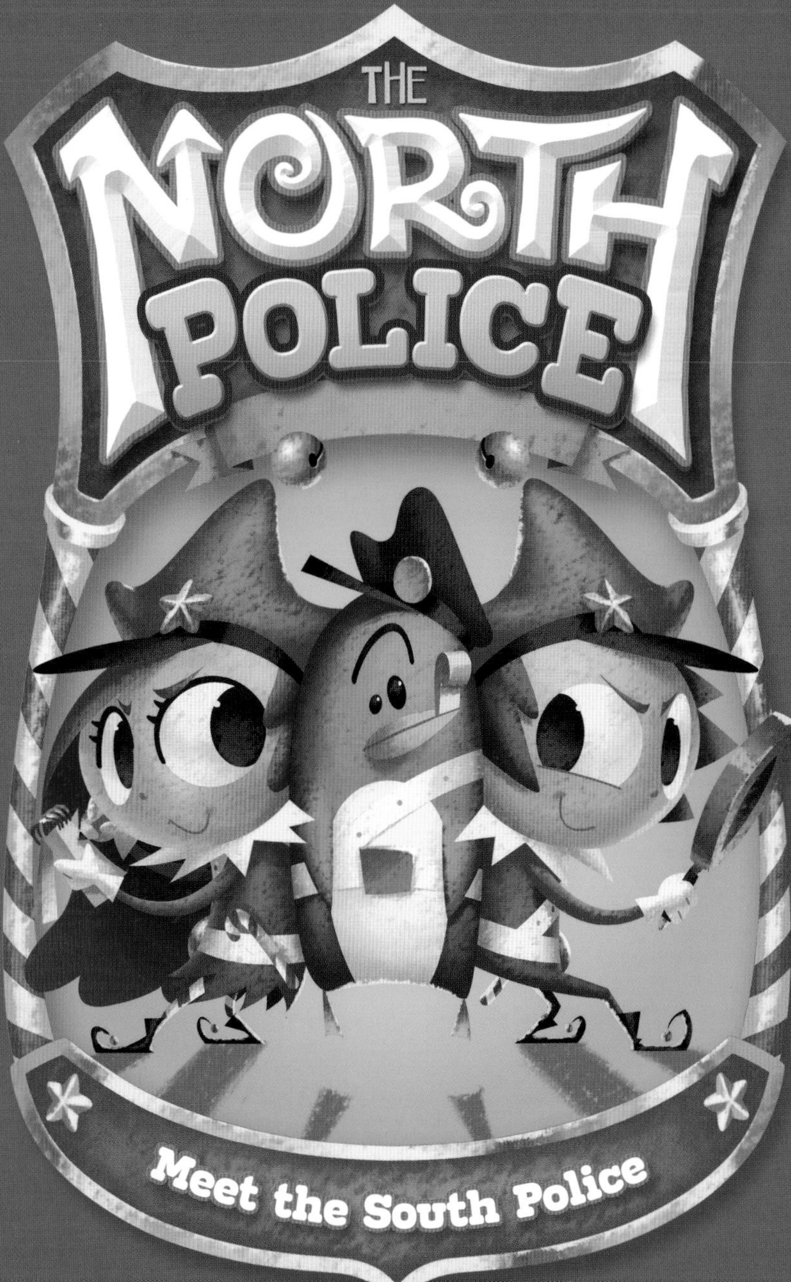
THE
NORTH
POLICE
Meet the South Police

CHAPTER 1
Missing!

Detective Sprinkles of the North Police rushed into the chief's office.

"Detective Sugarplum is gone, sir," cried Sprinkles. "She's been missing all day!"

"That's because she's on vacation," replied the chief.

It was the day after Christmas. After working so hard on December 25, many elves had taken the day off.

"But what if there's trouble?" Sprinkles worried. "I've never solved a case without a partner."

"You won't have to," said the chief.

"The South Police sent one of their best officers to fill in," the chief explained.

The South Police officer waddled into the room.

"HONK!" he said.

Sprinkles leaned over to the chief. "Sir, that's a penguin," he whispered.

"Of course," said the chief. "That's who lives in the South Pole!"

"All the best officers in the South Police are penguins," the chief added.

"HONK!" agreed the penguin.

Suddenly, the police radio on the chief's desk squawked.

"There's trouble on the Christmas Town highway!" said a voice over the radio.

CHAPTER 2
Honk!

The Christmas Town highway was jammed with elves returning to the North Pole after their day off.

The tow sleigh couldn't get through to the trouble.

"No problem," said
Sprinkles. "I'll just use my
sleigh bell siren."

Sprinkles hit the button.
Nothing happened.

The siren was broken!

"How will we get through all this traffic?" said Sprinkles.

"HONK!" said the penguin.

"Great idea!" said Detective Sprinkles as the traffic moved out of the way.

Sprinkles and the South Police officer led the tow sleigh to the trouble.

It was Sugarplum! The ice road had cracked under her sleigh. She was stuck!

Suddenly, the ice broke! Sugarplum's sleigh fell toward the icy water below.

"Oh, no!" cried Sprinkles. "If she hits the water, she'll be frozen for sure!"

CHAPTER 3
Rescue!

Detective Sprinkles jumped onto the tow sleigh. He grabbed the tow rope. Sprinkles threw the rope to Sugarplum as she fell.

But he missed!

"HONK!" cried the South Police officer.

The penguin dove through the air. He grabbed the rope in his beak.

The penguin hooked the
rope onto Sugarplum's sleigh
as it dropped through the air.

Then the South Police
officer splashed down into the
freezing water!

The rope caught the sleigh just in time. Detective Sugarplum was safe!

But what about the South Police officer?

"HONK!" said the penguin as he popped out of the water. He was okay, too!

"That water is much too cold for an elf," said Detective Sprinkles.

"But for a penguin," Sprinkles added, "I guess the water is just right."

The tow sleigh pulled Sugarplum and her sleigh back onto the road.

"I knew you'd get here in time, Detective Sprinkles," Sugarplum said. "The North Police are always there when you need them."

"So are the South Police," added Sprinkles.

"HONK!" agreed the penguin.

The North Police smiled.

"Another case neatly wrapped!" they cheered.

CHRISTMAS CRIMINALS

Spike

AUTHOR

Scott Sonneborn has written dozens of books, one circus (for Ringling Bros. Barnum & Bailey), and a bunch of TV shows. He's been nominated for one Emmy and spent three very cool years working at DC Comics. He lives in Los Angeles with his wife and their two sons.

ILLUSTRATOR

Omar Lozano lives in Monterrey, Mexico. He has always been crazy for illustration, constantly on the lookout for awesome things to draw. In his free time, he watches lots of movies, reads fantasy and sci-fi books, and draws! Omar has worked for Marvel, DC, IDW, Capstone, and more.